We Could Write This Shit!

Hilariously Bad Sex Scenes

B. A. Loudon | K. Morrow

ISBN: 978-1-9990560-2-5

We Could Write This Shit! Hilariously Bad Sex Scenes

This book is a work of fiction and the product of the twisted imaginations of the authors. Any resemblance to businesses, events, vehicles, persons living or dead (or the living dead) is entirely coincidental. Though if any of the shorts remind you of a situation you've experienced, we'd just like to say – from the bottom of our hearts – we are so, *so* sorry you've had sex that bad.

Edited and arranged by B.A. Loudon. Cover by B.A. Loudon.

Acknowledgements

B. A. Loudon

To my son - may you never read this.

To my husband - thank you for not being an inspiration for this project.

To my mom – Hi!

K. Morrow

To every partner I have ever had, know you PROBABLY weren't the inspiration for any of these stories.

To my mother, who is always so supportive of my "little art projects."

To all of the readers, I thank you for putting up with my crass and dark humour. All I wanted was to make you laugh.

To that nice man that brings me food, and sometimes touches my butt, you rock a lot.

Introduction

If you've read the back cover, you already know what you're in for with this book. However, I don't need a reason to talk more about this book!

We love reading bad sex scenes. Who doesn't? They're especially great when they're unintentionally hilarious. Bad anatomy, clunky dialogue, weird analogies, - the list just goes on and on.

Over time, we realized that a lot of the above happened frequently. They're like the tropes of bad sex scenes. You could practically play Bad Sex Bingo with them!

With me being an English Major, and Kristen being both hilarious and creative, we decided to combine our powers to write the worst scenes we could. A lot of laughter and some revisions later, this book is the end result.

In this book you'll find two sections: Quickies, and A Bit of Foreplay. Quickies are our 1 page blurbs. Read it on the go, in the bathroom, wherever you might need something short but sweet to read. A Bit of Foreplay are longer, but still generally quick reads.

We sincerely hope you enjoy reading it as much as we did writing it.

- B. A. Loudon

Contents

Quickies

For when you're short on time.

Satisfaction not guaranteed.

Raiding the Fridge

Is this a love scene or lunch?

He inhaled her scent deep into his lungs. Her hair smelled of sweet strawberries and was as intoxicating as wine. He brushed her dark chocolate hair from her face; how had he gotten this lucky?

"What?" She asked, her voice smooth like a silky, melting ice cream.

"Nothing," he murmured back. "Just admiring."

Her body was perfect, laid before him like a spread of sweet desserts that he couldn't wait to sample. She looked delicious. Everything from her perfect, round cantaloupes to her lower halved peach called to his senses.

Her buns had his baguette fully baked.

He pressed her cherry lips to his.

Their bodies were warming together like a preheating oven. Everything about her was roasting him like a slab of raw beef and cooking him to absolute perfection.

"I'm ready," she gasped, her voice like a whistling tea kettle, and baby, it was tea time.

He was *very* ready to place his fully cooked, plump and juicy jumbo sausage between her steaming sesame buns to create the perfect, sexy hot dog.

Low-Key Bestiality

I'm not saying she wants to fuck a horse... but she wants to fuck a horse.

She took a moment to take his image in to her adoring, lustful eyes. Her heart leapt at the mere sight of him, especially as all of him was present before her. It was like they were at auction, and she was examining his features in great detail and admiration.

He was tall and majestic, much like a Clydesdale, and his spirit like a wild stallion; he was both powerful and graceful, untamed and alluring. The arms holding her were as strong as a thoroughbred, and freckled like a paint-splattered Appaloosa. Every move he made was smooth and sophisticatedly controlled, like the gait of a Tennessee Walker. She gently ran her hand through his hair; it was thick and luscious, like the mane of an Andalusian.

His muscles rippled beneath his skin, like a horse trotting leisurely; effortless, but beautiful. She imagined his long, silken neck looked as sexy and as elegant as a wild horse drinking from a stream whenever he drank. Her fingers entwined with his - even his hands were manicured, and reminded her of fine hooves. They were well used, worked hard, but well cared for and it showed in every detail.

He was magnificent. The perfect specimen of a man.

It was as though he was thoroughly bred for this; to be hers, and hers alone, forever.

He was a horse everywhere.

Everywhere, that is, except where it mattered.

The Zoo

Where did all these animals come from?!

She was like a beautiful swan; graceful and elegant, and all neck. He watched her hungrily, like a tiger eyeing his next hunt. She was his favourite prey, and he couldn't wait to eagerly devour every inch of her.

Her lips parted, and she let out a soft giggle. It was music to his ears, like a nightingale's song. He sometimes couldn't believe that he'd found her in this life - he still found her to be so exotic, like a giraffe in the wild. Her skin was almost soft to the touch, like a chinchilla's fur.

When their lips met, it was as if they were once again kissing for the first time. God, how many years had it been now? He wasn't sure - her intoxicating kisses wiped his mind of thought. The two of them were like beavers - bound to each other and only each other for the rest of their lifetimes.

It wasn't long before their passion for each other had them rolling around and grunting with the other like a couple of happy barnyard pigs in mud.

Her hands took to his boxers, and slid them down quickly. His member emerged like a proud slug, and stood looking like a naked mole rat.

It was time to get wild.

Be a Good Sport

Go hard! Touch the ball! (Balls?) Sports!

The music in the club swelled, and he imagined the chattering and shouting voices around him were the crowd cheering him on. It didn't matter that they weren't actually. What mattered was that finally, he would be a benchwarmer no longer; his time to get in the game had come.

He had spent years waiting for this, but they were not years wasted. Studiously, he had studied writing, photos, film… everything he needed to prepare for his first home game win.

Playing had been harder than studying, but it was going well. Early innings were spent chatting, drinking, and soon, tipsy flirting. The game shifted soon to can, with both teams fighting for dominance in the back seat. They were playing hard, breaking a sweat and desperately out of breath by the time they reached his apartment.

He had won two bases by the time they'd gotten through the door. Now, there were two balls in play and his pole was ready for vaulting. Her nets were wide open, ready for him to take his best shot with his stick.

He swung his club and nailed a hole-in-one on the back nine.

Touchdown.

Too Clinical

It's like an unsexy doctor's appointment.

He parted my labia with an intense precision.

Adam kneeled between my legs and stared down at my vaginal region. His phalanges moved inwards, towards the clitoris. I could see his penis getting hard beneath his jeans. How I wanted to free him from his denim pants. I longed for our genitals to meet. To be joined, like lock and key, penis in vagina.

I could feel my glands thrust into overdrive, my vaginal fluids running down my buttocks, gathering on the sheets. I leaned forward and grasped his pants, popped the button with my thumb and pushed the waistband down over his gluteus maximus, freeing his massive erect penis.

His body met mine, budding passion now exploding like white heat behind my eyes. He entered me, his penis in my vagina, and it became slick with my juices. He moaned as his eyes rolled back like a man possessed. Neurons fired rapidly, bringing us closer to the best scientific conclusion life had to offer.

I reached my hands back and grabbed his buttocks firmly before plunging a finger into his brown pleasure hole and sending him into complete orgasm.

That's Not How Orgasms Work

Like, at all.

His manhood pushed into my mouth; it was large, and the upper curve of it bumped the back of my throat. I worried that if he wasn't careful, he might end up fucking my brain. He moaned loudly and grabbed a handful of my hair, and pulled me even further onto his dick - if that was even possible. He was throbbing so powerfully in my mouth. I aroused him like no one else had, it was written all over his face. My tongue danced devilishly over his most sensitive areas. I had him. I knew it. He knew it.

I wasn't very good, but I seemed to have had an effect on him. He grabbed my hair and rhythmically pumped into my mouth. I had to concentrate on not dying as he was certainly taking my breath away, literally and figuratively.

I had wanted this so long, tried everything to make it happen. It was more than I had hoped. I was so turned on I might burst into flames! Feeling him rigid in my mouth, his hands wrapped up in my hair. I could hear him moan, I knew he was getting close.

Then I began to feel...*was that what I think it was?*

Yep, my own pleasure, bubbling up under the surface. Like a bottle of the cheap sparkling wine he had gotten to make this moment more special, my cork was about to pop. I dug acrylic nails into his thick thighs, and hung on for dear life. He was fucking my face and that was all I needed. A powerful orgasm rocked through me. I could feel myself melt; my eyes rolled back and I got the sweet, blissful release.

I Wonder if a Man Wrote This

Certainly wasn't written by a woman.

She laid before him, breathless and panting, naked and so exposed.

He looked her over. Her body was perfect. Neck? Perfect. Legs? Perfect. Arms? Perfect. Hands? Perfect. Knees? Perfect. Torso? Perfect.

Breasts? She had them, and they were perfect. They were round and caught the sunlight, enhancing their roundness like two boob coloured baseballs. They were great, just the best.

From the bed, she looked up at him with anticipation. He made her so wet that the bedsheets beneath her were positively soaked. His cock was large and hard, the largest and hardest she'd ever seen.

His body was great, he was toned everywhere and had a six-pack. No, wait, the light reflected off his oiled and well-tanned skin – could it be? An eight pack!

Her trembling vagina gushed once more.

He was certain that she'd be so tight, like a sexy lobster claw grabbing his dick. He dipped his hand down and pressed her clit; he only needed to ring the devil's doorbell once to send her into an intense orgasm, the most intense one she'd ever experienced.

He was great at sex.

Periods

For both punctuation and women, it's better when they're not missed

She kissed him breathlessly and pressed their bodies together in a sudden rush of boldness - which was entirely unlike her - but he responded enthusiastically, in both body and emotion, and it wasn't long before he was pulling away at her clothes and leaving them to wrinkle in heaps on the floor while the two of them became entwined on the bed in a fevered, passionate frenzy with hearts beating furiously and wildly; it was as if they were in sync, a perfect harmony of natural instincts, doing exactly what they were designed to do, whether by a god of some sort, if such a god existed, or perhaps just by the random chance of the universe itself but just like the majestic and powerful lions, to wild and untamed bears, to the lowly domesticated dog and its owners leg, so too were they boning, and boning hard.

A Bit of Foreplay

For when you've got some time to take it slow.

Satisfaction still not guaranteed.

Zombies

He let his lust overtake him, if he was looking for brains, he wasn't going to find them here.

Victoria stumbled through the graveyard. She wasn't sure if she would find him here, but she had to try. There were rumours whispered in her classes… Rumours of a creature.

She was nervous; she had never done anything like this before, but her 21st birthday was coming up and she needed to do something crazy. What if she died never having experienced anything in her whole life? She pulled her denim jacket tighter and held the flashlight as she wandered through the graves. Most of them were dirty, worn, and unreadable.

She finally arrived at the mausoleum. Legend had it that this was where *he* would appear. She paused, looked around to make sure she wasn't being followed, and finally pushed the heavy door open. The mausoleum was dark, the air was musty and smelled of wet stone, and decay. Silence rang in her ears; she was alone. She had to stay until exactly 3 AM. She made herself comfortable on a relatively dry spot on the floor, and waited.

Minutes ticked by. Maybe this was a mistake, what was she getting into? She was just about to let her nerves get the best of her when there was a creaking noise behind her. She felt a shiver come over her, and she smelled him before she saw him. She realized the musty, wet rotting smell was coming from *him*.

There he was, dark and mysterious, shrouded in mystery. His skin was a greyish blue tinge, matching his silver eyes, and his hair wild. He stood there, looking at her. At least, she thought he was looking at her. She couldn't really tell due to the lack of lighting, and the cloudiness of death over his pupils.

"It's you," he growled. She gulped. She tried to subdue her fear but it wasn't working. She took a step back. As if he could read her mind, his voice croaked, "Don't run, you know you want to stay."

Her back met the door, as he took a step towards her. Victoria's hand grabbed for the door handle but the door wouldn't move. Stuck. She was stuck. He put his hands on either side of her head and looked into her eyes. They stared at one another. She felt her fear melt away and began to feel heat in her stomach.

Faster than she could think, one hand grabbed her by her blonde hair and one arm wound around her waist.

"What did you come here for? Don't you know I'm a monster?" His breathe swept across her neck, making her tingle.

She grabbed his arms and felt the remaining muscles beneath them. He began to nuzzle her neck. Deep down, she knew she could be in danger, but she *needed* this. She needed *him*.

She gave his bulge a gentle pat, mindful of the fact that she wasn't sure which, if any, parts were detachable.

"How is this possible?" She asked, breaking her trance for a brief moment. "I mean, if you're… not living…" Victoria trailed off, flushing as embarrassment at her own train of thoughts took over.

"Embalming fluid," he growled, clutching her closer to his decaying body.

They embraced each other tightly as they fell to the floor. He rolled, pinning her beneath him. As his hands moved onto her chest to undo her sweater, her hands worked his remaining scraps of clothing at his waist. Once they were both sufficiently naked, he pulled her up from the stone floor, and laid her on the raised platform in the center of the room. His stone coffin, she realized. Empty, unlike she was about to be.

They shared in each other's passion. She rolled on top of him and giggled as she wrestled his arms above his head. He inhaled sharply and she let go of his arms, and the right one fell to the ground. Victoria was both mortified and horrified. He looked shocked.

This made things a bit more complicated, but not impossible. It could have been worse, they both mused silently.

"I-I'm sorry," she whispered as her face began to flush.

He jumped off the stone table and bent down to grab his rogue appendage. It was obvious there was no quick fix. He growled, and put the arm down on the square table.

"We can find a use for that later," he teased, getting close to her body again. He kissed her hard. He was a monster but she was feeling like this was heaven. "You have to play nice."

Though the smell was off-putting, she was absolutely intoxicated. She wasn't sure if it was a cocktail of her fear and excitement. Or him. She clawed at him, careful not to pull off any flesh. He let his lust overpower him. Changing her wasn't a priority for him right now. He needed her to feel how powerful he was. He drove into her. He was dark, dangerous, but she felt good to be with him.

As one hand worked and teased her, getting her ready for his member, the other took a handful of her blonde curls and caressed them. He kissed her deeply. His tongue explored the caverns of her- *wait a minute-* he only had one hand attached?! As his mouth moved to explore her neck, she shifted to sneak a peek.

His free arm working solely on its own, gave a gentle tug to her hair. Panic filled her. The rogue arm was participating, acting as though it had a mind of its own. She didn't have time to lose her shit, because her orgasm crested, bring heaven and hell together in one room.

The Perfect First Time

Because first times are always great. Always.

Ashwynn flushed in the soft candlelight. The dancing flame lit her face with a gentle glow, adding to her natural beauty. "I... I have a confession," she said shyly, "I've never done ...this... before."

The eighteen year olds had been suddenly caught up in a wave of passion, and looked at each other with a breathless hunger. Their clothes lay heaped in a pile on the floor of the otherwise immaculate room - her matching lace bra and underwear and his skills boxers sitting on top of the pile like a crown. It was all very spur of the moment, but it was all encompassing - perfect, as though planned.

Tom licked his lips.

"I haven't either," he admitted sheepishly to her as the soft jazz music surrounded them. The smooth melody of a saxophone warmed their newly naked bodies. The sensual trombone stoked their fires even hotter.

This was it. Their first time. Together. That special gift they could only give once, and they were giving it to each other. No one else.

"Really?" She asked softly as he laid her back against the rose petal covered bed. Where had they all come from? She decided that she didn't care. They were soft and silken against her bare skin.

He nodded. The strong fragrance of her perfume filled the already music and tension laden air. "You ready?"

She nodded back. He looked her deep in the eyes as he pushed his impressive length into her in a single, fluid motion and filled her fully. She gasped in pleasure; she had never felt this perfectly complete before, this full and satisfied. They were two perfect puzzle pieces, joined together for a perfect fit in body, heart, genitals, and soul.

It perfectly only then made perfect sense that when they came, they came in perfect unison.

I Don't Think You're Actually Into This

Your words say you are, but your descriptions say you're not.

The room wasn't really anything special - average, really, if one was being honest.

The curtains hung limply from the brass coloured rod. It wasn't even real brass, she had inspected it when her curiosity got the better of her; it was simply wood painted to look metallic. Why? Perhaps the owners thought it made the room more elegant. In reality, it just added to the pay-per-hour look one expected from a motel like this. The lifeless, cream coloured curtains had seen better days. Probably cute, white, and in their prime ten years ago, they now were just sad.

The same could be said of the carpet. Sure, it was clean enough, recently vacuumed. It wasn't as if it hadn't been cared for. Still, there was a discoloured spot near one of the queen sized beds - mostly likely coffee thanks to the small machine included in the room for your convenience. Occam's razor after all; the simplest answer is usually the correct one.

The imagination led one to wonder what other substances it could be. Urine? Gross, but possible. Blood? Had there once been a murder? Not impossible in a place like this. She wondered if it would be possible to get the grisly details. Was that something the desk clerk could legally disclose? The saying went "if walls could talk," but really, carpets could tell disturbing tales too, she mused.

The kitchenette in the corner by the ensuite bathroom was quaint, adorable even. The appliances – fridge, microwave, and the offending coffee pot, not much but at least the fridge was full sized - were old, but not so old they were completely outdated. Ten years, maybe? Fifteen? Old, but ultimately acceptable, and still functional. That was about all that could be asked of a place like this. Everything was mostly white, a bit of discolouration here and there, but more importantly like the rest of the room, they were clean.

The cupboards had scratches and wear into the wood, but they were real wood. That was more than could be said about some newly built apartments she had been looking at. When had vinyl covers with a wood pattern become a thing? Obviously after this hotel had been built. It was really a shame. Not that the craftsmanship was wasted here, but she felt that it should be somewhere it would be better appreciated.

And then there was the wallpaper. The wallpaper really tied the room together like the icing on an average, mediocre but somehow still enjoyable cake.

Dated, but not unpleasant. The pattern was a light, faded floral. The intention was probably to make the guest feel more at home, as if they were in the guest bedroom at their grandmother's house. Sure, it's not your house, but it's comfortable and non-threatening - You feel safe enough to sleep through the night, and that was really the best measure of a room, wasn't it? The ability to sleep soundly. She noted that since the wallpaper hadn't been changed out in some time, and there were no obvious signs of blood spatter, there likely hadn't been any murder.

That is, with the exception of the man on top of her who was murdering her pussy savagely into the bed. She'd never experienced such intense, all-consuming pleasure with a man before. Her every sense was overwhelmed and consumed by him, and only him, and the dicking that she was happily receiving.

Trying but... So Unsexy

So unsexy it hurts

He led her by the hand through his expansive home. Her eyes darted from place to place, trying to take in her surroundings.

"What a beautiful home you have. What is it you do again?" She said in between dodging his pecks.

"Finance," he muttered as he pulled her closer to him. She could believe that fact; he had the personality of someone who worked in finance.

She looked at him in the glow of the living room lights. He looked delicious, and not just because she could see the stain from the hot wings they had shared over dinner around his mouth..

Chicken bones weren't the only thing she would be sucking on tonight.

Suddenly, he pushed her back onto his couch. The hard padding met her back with a dull thud. He sat down beside her and looked into her eyes. His hand hovered over her crotch, and he gave her a gentle pat there to remind her of his intentions.

She could no longer keep her hands to herself, and she jumped onto his lap. She wrapped her arms around his neck and he greeted her with an over eager, open-mouthed kiss. He lapped at her, the way a dog laps at water on a hot summer day.

This would be the first time she would see him naked, she realised with a shiver of excitement. Patience be damned! It was time for caution to be thrown to the wind. She hurriedly tore at the buttons on his shirt and slid it from his shoulders. When she saw his bare chest, her breath caught in her throat. His non-existent muscle mass was evident, and his pale flesh reflecting the light from the lamp. How she loved a strapping man, but she would have to make due for tonight.

Her hunger filled her, she could not wait.

His tongue darted in and out of her mouth while his large hands perused her body, stopping only briefly to handle her generous melons. No sooner had he grabbed her blouse and ripped it off than his fingers began to search for the clasp of her bra. He fought to free her from her clothed prison.

"Be free" he whispered triumphantly as it finally came apart.

She ran her hands over his ribs, her fingers mimicking a xylophone, she chuckled at this in her head. They freed themselves of all of their clothing. She let her gaze pass over her partner. All she saw was bones, bones....*boner...*

The Perfect Body

What a man really wants.

Steve looked out the window onto the street, watching the traffic go by. Ever since the accident, he felt uneasy around cars. How could he not? It had changed his life forever.

He watched life go by; everything was different, but nothing had changed. Time had marched on. The sun rose and fell. His mail still fell through the slot in the door. The paper got printed, delivered. Everything was the same, save for one thing.

She wasn't here anymore.

Cara and Steve had been together for three years. Markedly the best years of his life. His chest tightened as he try to pry his thoughts from his beloved whom now only existed to his memories and his imagination.

So what, I can think about her if I want to, I'm coping.

He went to his couch, the faded fabric received his weight as he sunk down, lost in his memories.

He could remember everything about the day he had first seen Cara. She wasn't a rich man's beauty, but she was his kind of lovely. She was simple and understated, so much so that he had almost passed her by. What a shame that would have been, wouldn't it? Despite all the pain, he knew he wouldn't have traded their time together for anything.

Her frame petite. Her pale complexion. He could remember it all as if he were reliving it.

He almost choked.

Brad had introduced him that fateful, he recalled. Brad had led him over to her so he could, as Brad put it, could "kick the tires." A crude statement to make about such a fine lady, but typical Brad.

Steve felt guilty remembering her like this. It would be a lie to say it was love at first sight. Much more like second sight, possibly even third. It didn't matter now... She had taken him by storm.

Their relationship grew dramatically over the next year. She was so trustworthy, and laid back. She made everything feel so easy. Nothing Steve could do seemed to bother her much, as long as he kept his promises to her. And he had, gladly.

Sleep grabbed him and pulled him under where his dreams began to reminisce about their *first time* together.

Steve had been working in the garage with Cara when he realized that they were completely alone... Just them, and the stillness. She was as she always was; calm and still, but an energy about her like she could go from 0 to 60 if the right things were done.

This was the moment that their growing attraction had finally reached its boiling point, his mind recalled. Not that he hadn't thought about her that way before then – fantasized about her, even – but neither had been ready to act.

Until then.

He used this moment as he began to slowly tease her. To his surprise and delight, she didn't shy away from his touch. Though she remained still in place, there was a playfulness about her. It lingered in the air

He slowly traced the tips of his fingers over her curves. She had a lot, and every one of them was perfectly placed. Touching her like this was exhilarating; he could feel his pants tightening. It was as if she had been perfectly – no, *divinely* – designed.

Fortunately, he knew exactly how to turn her on and get her motor running as hot as she made his, and it wasn't long before Cara was humming under his touch. It was glorious. She had him so worked up that he could barely contain himself.

Eventually the teasing became too torturous. Unbuttoning his pants, he hurriedly grabbed himself. He worked himself until he was fully hard, all the while imagining how she felt inside. When they were both fully ready for one another, it was like wild horses running free. 110 horses to be exact, her like 109, and him, a wild stallion.

He remembered the cool steel of her frame touching his most intimate part. He would let her be on top, submitting to her desires. He slid under her and began working himself to frantically completion. Steve couldn't hold on anymore. Electricity fired through him. He felt her engine vibrate powerfully above him like a goddess, and with a sudden rush, he was over the edge. His moans echoed off the walls of the garage as he came harder than he had ever before.

Steve awoke with a start in a cold sweat. Why was his mind so cruel? Dreaming only reminded him that she was forever gone, forever separate from him. His heart ached desperately for her.

He would never again be with his beloved hatchback.

About The Authors

B. A. Loudon

B. A. Loudon is a Canadian writer. She has been writing consistently since she was fourteen and loves to write all genres. Her biggest influences are dry, British comedy, and True Crime.

She likes to think that she's witty. Sometimes she actually is.

B.A. Loudon enjoys travel (especially music cruises), spending time with her husband and their young son, and believes life is too short to not be happy in what you're doing.

Find her online at baloudonwrites.com

K. Morrow

K. Morrow is a Canadian actress and writer. Acting is her passion and she hopes to one day make it her full time job.

K. Morrow loves her family, makeup shopping, and thinking up the darkest jokes that she can.

Find her on Instagram: @KLM_orr

@that_shadelife for her make-up finds and looks.